The

Awakening

A Story Of Unconditional Love
And One Life Changing Gift

Sam Spencer

Illustrated by Ken Corbett

Copyright © 2011Sam Spencer

ISBN-10: 1938091000
ISBN-13: 978-1-938091-00-1

theawakening@samspencer.us

www.samspencer.us

CONTENTS

Dedication

This book is dedicated to all those who struggle with life's challenges. Each one of us surely fit into this category. To those dreamers who search and find greater fulfillment.

Sam Spencer

A Note From The Author

Dear Reader.

Very early one morning I woke up after an interesting dream, the clock on the dresser read three o'clock; it was just too early to get up. Soon I found myself mentally completing the story waiting to fall back asleep. As I lay in bed expanding on the story line I thought to myself, "this is a great story, you should get up and write it down!" I was just too tired and cozy in that warm bed resting under my plush covers. I figured that I would make some notes in the morning. It didn't take long until I fell asleep once again.

For a second time I awoke after repeating the same dream. The characters were the same and as I recall the story appeared to also be the same yet more vivid. A few of the phrases were verbatim and now had fixed themselves firmly in my mind. I lay in bed mentally adding detail and embellishment. As I lay in bed pondering the verbalized phrases the story seemed to unfold before me. With more intensity I kept repeating to myself, "get up and write this story down! This is a great story! You will forget it!" Once more sleep overcame me.

Again for the third time I had the same experience as twice before. "I've got to write this story down," I kept saying to myself. I laid in my comfortable bed, wrapped up in a warm blanket, lying on my back, my pillow perfectly supporting my head. I kept developing the story, the images formed in my mind as if I had actually lived it. "I've got to get up," again I urged myself. At last I forced myself to get up. I sat down and started writing. From just before sunrise until after well after sunset I sat at my computer keyboard. The story just kept developing. More detail and explanation now flowed. It was almost like I had actually experienced it. Well, in my dream I had!

I am certain that as you read the following pages you will cry, you will experience anger and you will applaud. You will see a little of yourself in one of the characters questioning yourself, congratulating yourself. But most importantly you will see yourself with new direction, with a more defined vision of who you are and what you can become even as young Jonathan did in his story.

Read this story with your children and your friends. Discuss its life experiences and values. See yourself making decisions and choices. For truly we chart our own course each day of our life writing a quiet history by each action.

I believe that this story was a gift. Yes, it certainly was a gift to me. Gifts truly bring the greatest pleasure when shared. I share this gift with you, unconditionally, with no expectations and without qualifications. May this story in some way fill your life's cup with joy! May you find encouragement and peace. May you without encumbrance give more freely of your gifts to others, unconditionally, with no expectations and without qualifications!

Enjoy! And Share!

Sam Spencer, Author

Sam Spencer

Chapter One

My Heritage

My Heritage

Everyone has a story to tell. Some are exciting, most not so much. Some are interesting, others would bore you. Some teach us, some you don't even understand. Well my name is Jonathan Christian Grant, and this is my story. How unique or interesting, you will get to be the judge. I'm not sure if there is any thing you will learn from this tale, certainly that too will be up to you to decide.

Everyday I asked myself; "why me?" Why was it that a little boy like me had to have a life that brought me so many challenges and so much uncertainty? My real parents were good people, at least so much as I remember. Not very many memories are left, or maybe I have blocked them out because of the pain. It was a terrible accident that took their lives. I can't remember anything about that day but somehow I survived. There were many times I felt that it would have been better if I had joined them. I was barely six years old. What was I to understand about life? I was all alone, no place to turn, no one to love me. If that wasn't bad enough, my father was an only child and his parents too had passed on.

My mother had immigrated to the US when she was about 20 years old, she came from some war torn country in Europe. I'm not sure of any of the details. I'm not even sure which country it was and it probably doesn't really matter. However, she married my dad a few years later. I don't even have any pictures. I'm not even sure how my parents first met. No one can tell me one paltry detail about my heritage. I just know people said my mom spoke with an accent. They said that she was very pretty, but I have long lost the only picture that I once had of my parents. It just seemed that my life was going to be some kind of nothing.

Heritage, oh sure! What is this thing they call heritage? I'll tell you about heritage! I had no heritage! I had nothing! I didn't even have a trail of tears that lead from my sorrows! Who was ever around to wipe them if they were to fall onto my cheeks? Who was there to even see if my eyes might well up from the pain? Nobody, nobody I tell you! I don't ever remember crying, no not once. Huh, if you really want to know about my heritage, I'll tell you about my heritage. Here it is! Its real simple··· I was born. I was left alone. I lived, and someday I will die. There, you have it, that's my heritage! Just like my parents, one day I'll leave this world too; abandon everyone and everything that ever was a part of me and nothing will be left, no, not anything of value or consequence! This is how I felt growing up, and probably would have lived an angry, less than fulfilling life had I not experienced my great awakening. I never could have imagined the twists and turns my life would soon take, the people I would meet and the impact that they would have on me.

Let me continue with my story. After my parents died I was sent to an orphanage. That was supposed to be a real good thing! Now I was left to become just one of the many kids left to survive by whatever means possible. Sneaking food into your room. Hiding it not only from the warden, but also mostly from the other kids who would steal it in a minute. Someone else simply out of jealousy often would destroy any nice item that one might obtain. It was survival of the fittest, in the most cunning of ways and at times the cruelest. I learned to always watch my back. I trusted no one!

I spent many nights unable to sleep and while lying awake in bed I would fantasize what it would be like to grow up in a real family. I would imagine myself playing ball with my dad, helping him fix the car, laughing and staying up late on Christmas or even New Year's Eve. Oh yes, and always a hug and a kiss goodbye as I left for school. Maybe a short story at bedtime or even getting tucked into bed. I would imagine my mother baking fresh pies in the kitchen on a warm Sunday afternoon in the summer. I could see her calling my dad and me in from the yard were I was having the kind of fun sons have with fathers like playing catch, kicking a ball or simply playing tag. Together the three of us would be just sitting there and eating homemade ice cream and fresh baked apple pie. I loved pie and ice cream. What a treat! We never got much of that in the orphanage. At best we might get a cookie as an after dinner treat, but that was rare. You wouldn't dare save it or one of the bigger kids would make you give it to him. Fantasy was my salvation. My dreams were what helped me to survive the painful life of what seemed like an eternity in the orphanage.

There was very little privacy in that big building I was forced to call home. The building was quite old with very tall ceilings. I was told that it was built about fifty years ago specifically as an orphanage. There were lots of rooms on the second and third floors; this is where the children slept. The third floor was just boys and the second floor was just girls. An interesting thing about this building was that there was a stairway on one side of the building that went from the third floor to the main level and on the other side a stairway that went from the second floor down to the main level. There was no passage from the second floor to the third floor, you had to go to the main level cross all the way over to go and access the other floor. This was something I never did, there was nobody that I wanted to visit on the second floor··· I mean they were all girls over there! In addition, there was always a guard to keep people from going the wrong way, a 24-hour guard.

At night when all was quiet the water pipes would make weird noises this was very scary especially when the older boys would act creepy. They would say; "did you hear that Jonathan?"

"They're coming to get you. Watch out!" I would burry my head under my pillow and cover my ears until I would fall asleep. The windows to me were very tall and mostly the blinds stayed shut. The hardwood floors were noisy and cold. I think they made them that way so you wouldn't sneak around. Our rooms were small and most of the time you had a roommate.

I found that it was easier to keep to myself. I learned that a friend would soon be taken from you never to be seen or heard from again. The loss of someone close was something that I had experienced early in life and felt safe in keeping my distance. I guess you could say that I had built a barrier for protection. Plus friends seemed to always get you into trouble.

I can't tell you what the girl's rooms were like, but the boys had one large bathroom with several showers. Where was my privacy? I had none! I would often wait until the bathroom was empty to take my turn. This was quite a challenge when the orphanage was full.

My room was small with a bunk bed and two desks. We each had a footlocker. I always took or got the bottom bunk. I liked it. I felt like it gave me an element of control. I told myself that it was the best place to be if I ever needed to escape, or should I say if the opportunity ever came up. Actually that was something that I would never consider, those who ran away were severely punished and the worst kids would be sent to a detention center and never seen again. I wasn't sure what a detention center was and had no desire to find out. There was a large window with not much of a view, mostly other buildings. We had to ask permission to open the window and even then it only opened enough to get your hand through it. The rules were so strict and you were always so afraid of being punished so you kept them merely out of fear. One good thing about my room was the afternoon sun. Oh yes, it felt warm and calmed my day's frustrations. I often would sit at my desk doing my homework and watch the sun set in the evening, this was my get-away, there I could imagine almost anything. This was my main source of sanity.

From my perspective of today, having arrived to a very different place than I have ever anticipated I ask an interesting question; "If you knew what tomorrow would bring, would you act differently today?" This again you will have to decide. Think about it! Another thing I have learned from now that I see my past with hindsight is that with each decision you make today you can predict to some extent what your future will bring. Not always in real things but in attitude, outlook and happiness. I think it is perspective. Let me go back to my story.

Chapter Two

In and Out

In and Out

One day, at about seven and a half years old, I recall being called into the warden's office. We called the head master, the warden and the name fit. The place was like a prison with the tall ceilings and the old building. The main level had two offices, a mess hall and a game area; this level had bars on the windows that accented the imprisoned feeling.

I remember the walk to the warden's office; it was down a long narrow hall of offices. I think it was that way in case you decided to run they could catch you easily. The floor creaked real bad just outside his door so you couldn't sneak up and listen to the secret plans they were making for you.

There was a couple sitting on the sofa in the office. I had heard about this before. People would take you away from this place. They would make you work for them, and if they liked you, they would let you be a part of their family. If not you would be sent back. This had happened to several of the others around here. I can't call them friends because you never were together long enough to become such. Yep, my suspicion would soon be proven right. There they were, a man and a woman, husband and wife, smiling at me with their big plastic smiles.

"Johnny," the warden spoke, "This nice couple is Mr. and Mrs. Adams,"

How did he know they were nice? I was sure he had barely met them. They didn't look nice to me. Mr. Adams had a long bushy beard. He was taller and bigger than the warden, I wouldn't say he was fat but he was a big man. He looked like a bear. His hands were huge, they looked rough and mean. That was scary. I could imagine him hitting me with those big mean hands. Some of the kids had told me stories of people hitting them, they told me how much it hurt. But that was nothing compared to his voice, it was deep and loud. He roared like a lion and he did most of the talking. He was wearing a brown suit that seemed quite uncomfortable to him. I guess it was all they could find that could fit him because he was so big.

Mrs. Adams was of an average height and size for a woman. Not too fat not too skinny, just average. She wore a long dress with a tan sweater. From her hair to her shoes she was plain, nothing special stood out. She didn't speak much, but she did have a pleasant smile. She kept smiling at me like she wanted to be my friend. I wasn't going to smile back, no way! I didn't want to give any indications that I was the prefect prey for their hunt.

"Johnny, Mr. And Mrs. Adams would like to let you live with them for a while," he continued.

"Let" me live with them?" I thought, as if they were running my life already. I asked myself; "how should I act? Should I act surprised?" Surprised that anyone would want me? Grateful? I could say, "Oh, what a surprise, and to think that *you* would want me!" Better yet, I think grateful would be best. Yes, grateful to get out of this prison to "freedom," if such a thing like freedom actually existed. Then I should fall on my knees and cry at their feet, "thank you, thank you, thank you for saving me from this awful place." Oh no! I thought, perhaps they would be moving me to an even worse prison. Who knows? Or maybe I should act as though I was so privileged. Privileged to be chosen for this experiment? I could stand with dignity and say, "This is such an honor that you would 'let' *me* live with you, how can I ever show you my gratitude?" I knew that this was the first step to slavery, a new life of servitude I would soon be sold to the highest bidder.

"Say 'how do you do, I'm pleased to meet you,' Johnny", the warden instructed, "go ahead you can say it now ⋯ and say it politely."

I hated it when anyone called me "Johnny," My real name is Jonathan Christian Grant. I only allowed my very few best friends to call me "Johnny," and the warden was certainly no friend of mine. Finally I swallowed hard and forced it out, "How do you do?" "I'm pleased to meet you." I thought I would be a smart aleck and add something extra, after all the warden was always telling us what to say, how to say it, and when to say it. If you even tried to say more or less you would be punished, which mostly would be being sent to your room without dinner. Yes this was perfect, this was my chance to ruin everything for the warden.

Here goes! "My name is Jonathan Christian Grant," I said enthusiastically as I sprang from my chair and vigorously shook their hands.

OOPS! Wrong thing... They liked it. The warden even made some kind of positively disgusting remark about me being quite friendly and easy to get along with. OH NO! My heart sunk. YUCK! I wanted to throw up. I just blew it! Not one more word did I hear from that point on, all I could think about was the thought of what might come. I was brought back to the world when I was finally dismissed and allowed to return to my room. I felt like the little puppy, being shown off to the neighbors so they could pet me, watch a few of my tricks then sent back to my kennel.

I found it difficult to sleep that night. How can you sleep when you think you might be torn away from what little you found to be secure and constant, and to make things even dreadfully worse, to be given away to some perfect stranger? I thought about running away but the stories of those who tried rang in my mind. But where would I go? I had no place to go, I had no one to run to and I certainly had no money.

I worried for the next two days. Then finally to my dismay the dreaded order from the warden came; "March down to the warden's office." There sat Mr. and Mrs. Adams. I felt my whole self tremble. Was this the end? Was I going to be shipped out like some homeless puppy from the pet store? My guess was sickening. I was given the bad news. Yes, I was going away. I slowly walked back to my room and began to pack my orphanage provided suitcase. Only if you were going to leave would they give you a few new things, otherwise they would give you only used items donated by sympathetic people. I got a new jacket! This was nice and took my mind off the trauma for just a moment.

Mr. Jones, one of the men who helped the warden with maintenance and odd jobs, watched closely as I completed this painful task. I guess they wanted to make sure I didn't take the bed or dresser because there wasn't much else in the room except for a big heavy army surplus desk and its chair.

This was pretty sad, all that I owned could fit into a suitcase and a small footlocker. The footlocker was filled with the few treasures that I had collected from Christmases and birthdays past. It made me real happy that they let me take my pencil and notebooks the school had provided me

I was on my way to a new and "exciting" life in the Adam's home. I still knew nothing about this family, but they thought they knew an awful lot about me. I'm sure the warden said whatever he needed to say to move me out. Actually there wasn't anything that I wanted them to know about me anyway. I had lost my family and I didn't need or want anyone else.

The ride "home" took about two hours. Mr. and Mrs. Adams talked to me all of the way home. They told me about their family; Mr. Adams, Mrs. Adams and the two children, one boy eight and a daughter 12. They also told me I would love them. I hated it when people told me how to feel. Was this going to be just like life with the warden? I can hear him now, in his deep loud voice; "Tell them your name, Johnny," "Tell them you feel fine Johnny." "Say 'please' Johnny" "Say 'thank you' Johnny." It never ended! What if I don't want to say 'please'? What if I don't want to say 'thank you'? What if I don't want anyone to know how I feel? They really don't care anyway. I guess I'll just cooperate and say "yes." Oh, I mean, "yes ma'am, and yes sir." That always worked with the warden, I'm sure it will work here too.

I sat and mostly listened, occasionally politely answering Mr. and Mrs. Adams' questions. The ride was great however from one perspective, it wasn't very often a boy like me was able to leave the orphanage and go on a field trip. Once we got past the tall buildings of the city the scenery was a lot of fun to watch. The trip was like going exploring without any hiking. The farms, the animals, the big trucks, everything was moving and changing. I especially liked the animals. We never were able to be around animals except when we were going to school we would throw rocks at the dogs and chase the cats. I had always wanted to pet a dog but the other boys who I walked to school with always threw rocks so I did too. Maybe the Adams would have a dog and I could pet it. Oh well, it doesn't mater anyway, they probably wouldn't let me play with the dog so I best not even think that way.

Finally we arrived at the city that was to be my new home. It seemed a lot smaller than where I used to live. No tall buildings and not as noisy. However, I guess that one place to sleep and eat is probably just as good as another. At least I wouldn't have to compete for food and space with so many people or be bullied into giving my treats away. Everything seemed to be at least satisfactory and to me satisfactory meant I could at least stand it. There really was nothing to "write home about," I mean if I had a home to write to. Like I said, life was just average.

Mr. Adams wanted me to call him "Father." How can I do that? "Father, Mother" I can't do that, I don't have a father anymore and I don't have a mother anymore. Didn't they tell him at the orphanage that my father and mother had died? Why did he think I was there? If I had had a father I wouldn't have been in the orphanage. This was a major challenge. Well, I only called him "Father" when I absolutely had to, and then I would force out the word, "Father." I didn't like that. It was so uncomfortable. I found creative ways to address him like "sir" or began a sentence indirectly so I could avoid calling him by that special title.

Now Mrs. Adams, well, she was actually mostly nice and on occasions I remember she asked me how I felt. This was new since I was accustomed to having everyone else who was a monarch over me telling me how I was supposed to feel. Perhaps she felt that I actually did have some feelings! Nevertheless I answered the way she expected me to answer, or at lest how I had been trained to respond at the orphanage.

Well, she wanted me to call her "Mom." Generally I did, "mom" was easier to handle plus she was not mean and demanding. At least that was better than being forced to call her "Mother," she sill wasn't my mother and never would be!

Life with the Adam's was nothing special. I just went to school helped with the dishes and did a few other chores. We watched approved TV programs but only on weekends. The children would play with me but when their friends came over I would go to my room and color and draw. Actually I didn't like them. They weren't my friends anyway. They were part of a real family; I was merely an unwanted guest, a freeloader. I never wanted to be there and I would never be a part of this family.

One thing that I enjoyed was our trips every Saturday morning to the library. I always checked out books with lots of pictures and illustrations. I would then reproduce them to teach myself to draw. When being sent to my room or playing alone I would draw. I loved drawing. Drawing made me feel free and independent creating whatever I was able to imagine. Imagination could take me anywhere and it was comforting to pretend that I was living my dreams. I could be doing everything that I could conceive. During these times I was the person in control. Drawing took me to my own private world.

Mr. and Mrs. Adams began to argue a lot. Mostly in the bedroom with the door closed. I think it was about me. Mr. Adams never was very friendly. I don't think he liked me. I'm not sure that he liked anybody. He would just tell everybody what to do and what to say. Then it finally happened. I knew that it would. Six months was all the Adams could handle of this arrangement. The experiment was over. They didn't want me anymore. I really wasn't too excited to go back to the orphanage, but one place still seemed to be as good as the another. Mrs. Adams drove me back. It was a long drive and few words were spoken. I didn't cry. I actually didn't care. As I said again and again: "I guess that one place to sleep and eat is probably just as good as another."

There were several new kids, but that was how it always was. The kids were in one day and out the next. Some never came back. Some of us did. It was hard to make real friends here because as soon as you got to know someone they would be taken away and never heard from again⋯ so why try? Everyone played and worked together but you kept your feelings to yourself. It was like being there physically but not emotionally.

By now I had adjusted to my life again. It seemed that my life went like this: Each morning I waited to get on the bus for school. I would come home and do homework. There were always a few assigned evening chores and then off to my room and then to bed just so I could start it over again tomorrow. I knew that if I just cooperated and didn't ask many questions that it all would be okay and I wouldn't get into too much trouble.

Well, I knew it would happen, and ultimately another family came to take me. I think that it was the warden's main job, to get us out into someone's home. This family was much the same as my first experience. It didn't last long. Shortly after moving in with these foster parents the father lost his job. He started doing odd jobs and would often come home drunk. He was impossible when he was like that, screaming, yelling, and even slapping and hitting people. When he came home we would all hide. I swore I would never touch alcohol or anything like that. I could see what a terrible monster drinking made of people.

Home life became so difficult that I was, in the end, sent back to the warden. Surely, once again, he would start looking for another couple to take me. By now I was a little past eleven years old. About all I had really learned was that if I waited patiently until my 18th birthday this would all end, jobs, money, freedom, and a car of my own. I imagined myself doing whatever I wanted and going wherever I wanted. These thoughts sustained me from day to day. "Six and a half more years," I would say, "Six and a half more years to freedom." I commenced my own private countdown. I envisioned that there was a light at the end of the tunnel, it was green and it flashed "EXIT." "Six and a half more years," I repeated.

Chapter Three

Mom And Dad

Mom And Dad

At last a good family that wanted me. The warden said that this would probably be my last chance with a family and told me to make the most of it and to do things right. I wondered why it was always *my* fault that things didn't work out. I had never chosen any of these families only the warden made those decisions. *He* was the reason for all the troubles. Yet *I* had to make his decisions work.

My new parents were kind of nice. They had no children so I would get lots of extra attention. Sometimes that was good and sometimes that was bad. No more sharing anything with the other children. What was mine would be all mine. No more "hand-me-downs." In the past everybody else had received new clothes, but for me just the leftovers. Oh no! The one thing I forgot, they would probably always be talking to me, I mean who else would there be? I wondered if I would ever be able to be alone?

The house was small but there were only three of us. It had three bedrooms and a single car garage. My bedroom faced east, that made it easier to get up in the morning. We were on a small farm with a barn where Mr. C kept a few animals. The little town was called Middleton. The address was 234 Grant Street. I hoped that this would be a good omen since Grant was my real last name.

Occasionally in the summer we went camping and fishing. This was a lot of fun. My dad worked a job in the city during the week and farmed about 15 acres on the weekends. Most every Saturday we would do chores on the farm. Fix fences, drive tractor, harvest the hay and whatever. In the winter there were fewer chores. Mrs. C had the extra bedroom set up for sewing and always had a quilt she would work on a little at a time. Several of her projects had won awards at the County Fair, however, most she would sell for extra money. A few she gave as gifts. She had a reputation for quality work. She always had someone waiting for something she was making.

Mr. and Mrs. C always spoke nice to each other and even to me. I was always able to go wherever they went. They kept me busy and generally worked on projects with me. This was nice since mostly in the past I was told what to do and if I didn't do it just perfectly I would get into trouble. I was not yelled at or punished unfairly. Life was good.

I recall that shortly after I arrived, Mrs. C made me a special blanket for my 12th birthday that was real nice and when I used it I always felt special. She was always doing things to make me feel important. Whenever her friends came over she would brag on me and show off my latest project and schoolwork. I liked the attention but didn't let on.

Still my only dream in life was for total freedom. The orphanage had taught me that life would begin when I was 18. Though I felt secure that's what I longed for. Perhaps this place would be satisfactory until I could move out on my own. I just lived a quiet uneventful life, year after year conforming to my surroundings. This was the safest survival method I knew.

I was soon to be sixteen! Exciting, I would then get my coveted drivers license. Yes, a right of passage. Society owed this to me and I was going to take it. This would be my first major step toward independence. This would allow me when age eighteen to drive off into the sunset and then be in control of my life. This also meant I could get a job, another important step, money in the bank! I could see the light at the end of the tunnel getting brighter and brighter it was still flashing "EXIT." The funny thing is that as I look back from where I am today, I now see that I always had much more control of my life than I ever recognized. I was blinded by my anger!

By now I had added painting to my drawing. Every art class in school found it's way into my schedule. In my room hung several ribbons along with the walls full of drawings and paintings. Mrs. C helped me enter several projects in the state fair and other contests just like her. With school and my part-time job at the airport it soon became very hard to find time to draw except when I was in art class at school or sitting in church. My parents made me go to church every Sunday. It was a nice quiet time though I saw little value in it. Oh! There was one good thing... what a great time to draw! And yes, the girls!

Summers around here were always busy. Between the summer chores on the farm and my summer hours at the airport I didn't have much spare time. We did have a standing family tradition however. The first Sunday of every month everyone would gather to have dinner at Aunt C's. Everyone brought part of the dinner. My dad and his two brothers would take turns making the customary home made ice cream while Aunt C would generally bring six or eight pies she had made on Saturday. There would always be leftovers that everyone would split up to take home. When it was dad's turn with the ice cream I would insist that he make strawberry vanilla, my favorite!

We would play all kinds of games, sit around and laugh at things everyone had done. Mom would often show off some of my drawings. This was always so embarrassing but in a way I enjoyed it. When the weather was good we would play softball, basketball or football in the large backyard. The children against the parents were always the greatest fun, especially when we won.

Sam Spencer

Chapter Four

Freedom

Freedom

It was my 18th birthday, the greatest day of my life, at least so far anyway. The first actual step to my freedom! I had planned for this day since way back in the orphanage. The final piece of this long awaited puzzle would actually take place in 2 ½ months, my High School Graduation. That would be the true day of my freedom! Only 10 more weeks until all my dreams would finally be able to come true. Jobs, money, freedom and I could buy a car of my own. How I had long looked forward to this day!

"Happy birthday'" Mom said as I walked into the kitchen for breakfast. "I've fixed your favorite breakfast · · · sausage, eggs and toast."

"Thanks, where's dad this morning?" I questioned. He usually ate with us before I caught the bus for school.

"He should be back in just a minute," mom replied. "He had to run to Bob's this morning, I expect him any minute."

Bob was dad's good friend; they had done a lot of work together at Bob's lately.   Just as I had settled in at the breakfast table dad walked in.

"Oh good, I'm not too late." He said excitedly as he took his place at   the   table.   "Happy Birthday Son. 18 years old, you're considered an adult now.   That should make you feel real good. After we finish breakfast Mom and I have a special present for you."

What's this?   Tell a boy on his birthday no less, that you have a gift for him and then make him wait?   I packed my breakfast down and waited for mom.   Mom was always slow but this morning she seemed to be even slower than ever. She must have enjoyed tormenting me. Her pleasant smile seemed to be hiding something.

"Hurry mom," I exclaimed impatiently, "I don't want to miss the bus!" It was still early, but the surprise, I wanted the surprise! Finally she was done, the dishes were gathered and out the door I started.

"Wait!" Mom stopped me, "Tie this towel for a blindfold, it's a surprise." Mom just loved surprises.

"Here, let me lead you," Dad continued as he took my arm and led me out to the side of the garage. He grabbed on to the blindfold and counted, "1 · 2 · 3."

"What," I yelled as the blindfold slipped away. "Is this for me?" My eyes were fixed on a finely waxed new car, well not brand new, but new to me!

"Yes," mom and dad both answered in unison.

Mom began to cry as I hugged them. She always cried in happy moments. "Can I drive it?" I asked. Now I knew why dad had spent so much time at Bob's the past several weeks.

"Of course," Dad answered, "The keys are in it."

"Can I drive it to school?" Again I asked, hoping for a yes.

"It's yours, we bought the first tank of gas, the rest are up to you," he added.

"Wow! Wow! This is great! Thanks so much." OOPS! Almost a tear of joy··· but not me, no way! "Thank you! What else can I say, but thank you again?"

I had never been so excited. My new independent world was opening up to me already. I recalled the day back in the orphanage when I started my countdown to freedom. That big green "EXIT" sign was getting closer. It was so close I could almost touch it!

Between school work and my part time job at the airport the weeks went fast. It was finally graduation day. This was the last obstacle in front of that exit sign. Now my position at the airport would become full time. Many opportunities would now be available to me. Soon my flying lessons would start. One of the instructors I knew at the airport made a special deal with me. I would help maintain his aircraft in exchange for private pilot lessons. Now my life was finally beginning to come together. It took me a little over three months but at last I got my private pilot's license. Most of my paycheck was spent on renting aircraft to get in my flying time. But it was worth all the work and every penny.

While working at the airport I became acquainted with several charter pilots as they flew in and out. I had many exciting conversations with them that motivated me to wanting to become a charter pilot also. One in particular was named Will. He seemed to have taken a liking to me. Will was part owner of North American Charter. He would tell me stories of how he and his partner had started their business about ten years ago with one plane and now they had several. About once a week he would have business in our area. Our conversations were particularly enjoyable for me because I wanted to be like Will and start my own company someday as well. This was part of my quest for real independence.

"I've watched you for several years," he said one day. "You are a good dependable worker. I wonder if you would like to come and work for us. You would act as maintenance and ground crew and if you would like to continue and get your commercial license, well, we could help."

"Are you offering me a job?" I exclaimed. I was so excited I felt like I was actually soaring in the clouds!

"Sure, you like this flying business don't you?" he asked.

"You bet I do. I really would like to move on and get my commercial license so I can fly for you." I answered. I didn't want to seem too excited and scare him but I was excited.

"First we would use you as maintenance and part of our ground crew," he continued "and let you learn all you can while we help you get qualified to pilot our aircraft." He started toward his plane and added, "Put some thought into what I have said and we can talk again next week."

The decision was easy; it was like a fairytale come true. A few weeks later I found myself packing most of my things into my car and I was heading for this great opportunity. It wasn't that hard to say goodbye. So many times I had gone through this sequence at the orphanage and for that matter with all the other families that had taken care of me. Most of my life was spent saying goodbye to someone. That's why it was safe not to get too attached. A few quick hugs, a kiss on the cheek from Mom, and a final wave as I drove off. Mom wiped a tear from her eye as dad said, "we're so proud of you son."

As I drove off I found myself feeling like I might miss them as I whispered under my breath, "thanks for taking care of me, it was great!" The old faded into new as I drove out of Middleton and before long Middleton had totally disappeared.

This was perhaps the most exciting day ever in my life. Freedom and independence! I was now in control of everything. It would take about eight hours to drive to the larger city that would become my new home. First check into a motel then find an apartment that was the order of business. Just think of it; in a few short years I could actually be flying for North American Charter. I would be somebody. Me, a pilot! WOW! I thought of the orphanage and the warden, what would he say now? I'm sure he would take all the credit. I'll just keep this to myself, this was all mine.

It wasn't easy. It seemed every spare minute was spent studying and working on becoming qualified to fly for North American Charter. The company required that I pay 50% of the cost of my schooling but I finally got it all done. Now I was able to fly as copilot with the regular pilots until they felt I as ready to handle routine excursions.

Moving up the ladder I finally became a solo pilot. I would always volunteer for any extra work that came up. I just loved flying. The words "where next?" was my perpetual question. I dreamt that some day I would have my own plane and do charters. It would take forever to get into that position. Maybe I could find a partner and we could start small as Will did.

North American had been my employer for almost 5 years now. I began to get restless and started to look at other flying opportunities. Then a help wanted ad especially caught my eye, "Corporate Pilot Wanted" it read, "two engine aircraft qualified," so far, I was qualified. "Monday through Friday, H & M Minerals." The office was about an hour drive away. I called and set up an appointment for the following week. This was exciting. I had never interviewed for a job before, I was nervous, but felt confident and qualified.

Chapter Five

The Company

The Company

The Interview seemed simple enough. I went in for my first interview on Thursday. When I left they said that they would make a decision in just a few days. On Saturday morning they called, "Can you come back on Monday?" Most certainly I could!

The second visit was brief and to the point. "You have been selected for this position," explained the personnel director. "How soon will you be able to start?"

"In two weeks," I returned, " I'll give my notice today, will that work?"

"That will be fine," he answered professionally.

I was dismissed and returned in two weeks ready for this new opportunity. My first day on the job I took two people to a small town. I waited for about four hours at the airport for the return trip. This job was not too difficult. It appeared I would spend a lot of time waiting so I began to carry a briefcase with a book to read and most importantly, my sketchpad. The first week literally flew by. Each day I had some new assignment. I babied my new plane; I would polish and clean it in my waiting time. I was told that I would be on call but that most of my trips would be during regular business hours.

Friday came quickly, the last day of my first week on this new job. It had been a good week. I was ready for the weekend. I had already begun to make plans to go camping and fishing nearby. This was beautiful country and I wanted to enjoy it.

My final assignment for the week seemed rather unusual. I was to fly a box of supplies to a ranch house. To me this seemed especially unusual since there was ground access and one could easily get supplies at the nearby town. My instructions were to leave at 12:30 and make the forty-five minute flight to the ranch house. I was to stay there until I was sent back and then my week was over. Great I thought, I could be on my way to the mountains by three o'clock.

At 12:30 sharp I took off and headed to the ranch house. It was a beautiful day in early spring. You could see forever. The wind had cleared out the haze from the valley. This was truly a great job. My flight plan was laid out perfectly. Soon I would see the windmill. Yes, there it was. The airstrip came into full view and finally the ranch house appeared just where I had anticipated. I had plotted my flight perfectly. The windsock was limp. I was ready to land. Here at last! A rush of adrenaline ran through my body fueled by my anticipation of what was here for me. I would shortly start the last leg of this trip and begin my well-planned weekend. This was great, I was in control!

As I landed a serene peaceful feeling came over me. I taxied my plane on the pavement to about 100 feet from the house. I shut down the engines, grabbed the box and made my way to the front door. This was a large house, log cabin style with a forest green metal roof. It was particularly picturesque in this mountain setting. There was a huge porch that wrapped the entire house. I noticed a wheel chair ramp leading onto the porch as I briskly ran up the stairs. I rang the doorbell and I heard a faint voice inside, I could not understand what was said. Again I rang the bell. A louder but gentle voice said, "Please come in."

Slowly I pushed the door open. Scanning the room from right to left. Then I saw her seated in a wheel chair. How would I describe her? If she were to stand I would guess her to be no taller than 5' 3". She was on the thin side, not fragile, but I would say delicate. She had what seemed to be naturally curly thick hair. From the pleasant expression on her wrinkle free face I would have guessed that the gray streaks in her otherwise dark hair were premature. She rolled the wheelchair over to where I stood, and pointed to the kitchen.

"Please put the box on the table," she said, " My name is Sarah Hollings, I'm pleased to meet you."

"My name is Jonathan," I answered. She was extremely pleasant and her demeanor seemed so disarming, I felt very relaxed. No body had ever made me feel so instantly comfortable. Or possibly I had never allowed it.

"Please have a seat," she pointed to the sofa, "You must be the new pilot."

"Yes," I responded. Now I wondered what happened to the other pilot? I would never ask. I was on a work assignment and would never ask such a question, yet my curiosity increased.

"I'm sure you will do well, you seem like a very nice polite young man." She continued.

"Thank you," I returned. It was nice she would say that, however, how does she know that I am a 'nice young man,' this is the first time we have ever met. How can you even know what someone is like when you have just met them?

"No, thanks to you for bringing my things," She responded. "I really appreciate your coming."

I really felt it, I could see it in her face and I sensed it in her voice, she was grateful but for what? All I had done? But it was my job. This seemed new, I actually felt appreciated. Her way of talking made me feel so comfortable. I had never talked to anyone who made me feel so much at ease. Who was this woman? I had so many questions. Why would I fly in a small box of 'supplies' and why leave at precisely 12:30? I could have come here this morning. What would she be doing? What was really in that box? What else was I to do? And, when can I leave? I now had remembered my weekend camping trip.

I scanned the rooms that I could see, there was no evidence that anyone else was home in this impeccably kept house. I wouldn't dare ask them but I sure had a lot of questions. What appeared to be family photos were placed around the house, who were they? Did she live here alone? I kept asking myself these and many other questions that raced by over and over again.

She again began speaking. "I love the beauty of Spring, everything becomes new and beautiful. It is a time when I think even nature is ecstatic with her own beauty. She seems to be getting dressed for the grand ball. I like to wheel my chair onto the porch in the morning and watch the sunrise awakening the world to a new day. A new beginning, a new opportunity to do great things, it's so beautiful. Then in the evening I like to go to the back porch and watch the sunset.

It's an excellent time for reflection, a time of gratitude for another glorious day."

"Sunrises are beautiful," I interjected. My thoughts sprang back to my little bedroom in Middleton where I enjoyed many a sunrise and then to the sunsets at the orphanage where I dreamt of my future. I was wondering if I could go now.

"I am so glad you like the sunrise, it can set the tone for the entire day," she said with an energetic smile.

"What if the sun doesn't shine?" I quipped.

"Oh, you just make your own sunshine," Again she started talking. She continued to speak briefly about sunrises and how they inspire her. "I am grateful for every day, and enjoy everyone I meet. I had a special treat today I got to meet someone new. I'm glad you came by and visited with me, it's been fun Jonathan."

"It has been my pleasure ma'am." I answered politely.

"Again, thanks for coming, I'll see you next week." She said as she rolled herself toward the door. " Be careful on your way home, and Jonathan, remember, *what you do for others makes you who you are.*"

"Thank you," I said cordially, and then quickly walked through the door toward the plane. Now I could finally return home. I looked at the clock in the plane, it was almost three o'clock. I had been there for over an hour and half. It really hadn't seemed that long. The time had passed so swiftly. The flight back to the hangar seemed to pass quickly too. I kept hearing her words, *"You just make your own sunshine."* -- *"You just make your own sunshine."* The visit left me with such a good feeling that it really didn't bother me being so late. All I could think about was how unusual yet comfortable the afternoon seemed to be.

Next Friday once again at 12:30 sharp I took off just as I had the week before and anticipated that this would become a weekly ritual. Since I knew the way I was able to enjoy the scenery more, the rolling hills covered with pine trees, the streams and lakes. I imagined that the fishing and hunting was really good in this area. I recalled the few times I had gone fishing and camping with my family. This certainly was beautiful country. I could surely understand why someone would want to live out here.

This week again I repeated this new ritual of delivering what seemed to be the same package. Was she going to keep me and talk to me for a while like the last visit? I guess it really hadn't been that bad. Just like last week I knocked on the door.

"Please come in," she answered again just as she did the previous week. "Please put the package on the table will you?"

I obliged with a "Yes ma'am," Then put the package in the same spot as last week.

"Thank you so much Jonathan," she said graciously, always making me feel so good, so accepted and so comfortable. "Will you please sit and visit before you return?"

"Yes Ma'am," I said once again, I really wasn't comfortable talking much, and I just wanted to be polite. I had no idea who this woman really was. I only knew that she had some connection with the company. Frankly I had no intention of being nosy.

Just then her dog came over to me. I hadn't seen him on my previous visit, but he certainly was well adjusted and friendly to strangers. He sat at my feet just inches from my knee. Waiting politely as if he were asking permission to touch me and to be touched, saying, "It's okay, you can touch me, please." I reached out and petted the top of his head. He scooted slowly forward and placed his chin on my knee as I stroked the back of his neck. Miss Hollings and I began to talk.

"What is his name?" I asked.

"Coco," She responded.

"What kind of dog is he?" I inquired.

"He is a mixture, mostly Cocker Spaniel, I guess. I found him lost and abandoned on the road several years ago and we have been friends ever since," she replied. "I have learned many lessons from watching animals, especially from dogs. You always know where you stand with them. Have you noticed how a dog will come up to you and ask permission to be petted? Everybody loves a friendly dog. And most dogs just seem to love everybody who is remotely friendly to them."

"I never looked at it that way," I said.

"Oh yes, we can learn something from dogs," she continued, "One important key to life that I have found is that people have to let themselves be loved. Did you notice how he came up to you with out qualification? He waited patiently for you to give him permission to love and be loved. We love them because they loved us unconditionally first. When you gave him permission he then gave you even more unconditional love back, no questions, willing to give you all he had to give for a single moment of undivided attention and unconditional devotion. Some people actually refuse to be loved." She continued, "I don't know if they feel unworthy or if they have been beaten down so much that they just refuse to love and to be loved"

"I guess," I answered as I tried to be a part of her conversation.

"If you truly want to be loved you must first love yourself and allow yourself to love others. You must give yourself permission to be loved." When she spoke these words it made sense. She went on, "People naturally want to be loved and want to love, but somehow there are those who loose trust in others and stop loving and letting themselves be loved. Sometimes it is something as simple as giving yourself permission to be loved."

This was getting to be a little too much for me. I had a hard time with all this love stuff. She went on talking more about her dog and this loving of oneself and loving others. She kept saying that they both are tied together.

Soon she began to roll toward the door. "Jonathan it has been a pleasant visit, thank you again and remember, *what you do for others makes you who you are.*"

"Thank you for your advice, it has been a pleasure." I remarked as I left for the plane.

As I flew home once again I found myself pondering our conversation. She had such a gentle way of speaking. She was quite subtle and relaxed. I just wanted to listen. She made so much simple sense. *"Give yourself permission to be loved,"* she had said.

I questioned myself; "Had I not allowed myself that privilege?" Was I one of the people she spoke of who are trodden down or that refused to let myself be loved? Was it so obvious that I had trouble loving others and possibly loving myself? Well, it certainly was a good visit and I was content with my new job, my new home and my new friend.

As the next week progressed work was slow and I spent a lot of time just hanging around the airplane. I was so excited that this was my plane, well just to take care of, I was proud of it and must have polished it a dozen times that week. I felt that there was no way that life could get any better than this!

Finally, Friday rolled around and again I found myself on the 12:30 trip to visit Miss. Hollings. When I landed I could see that she was wheeling herself around outside. The greeting was as usual.

"Hello Jonathan, It is so nice to see you. Please, just go into the house and put the package on the table, and thank you so much." When I returned she continued. "I wonder if you would help me plant these two lilac bushes, do you mind?"

"No of course not, I would be glad to help," I answered.

"Wonderful, would you please run around to the shed in the back and get a shovel?" she asked. "I'd like to plant them on each side of the front steps about three feet out. I want to give them lots of room to grow."

I returned with the shovel and she went on, "How do you like this new job?"

"It is great," I said excitedly, "I love it anytime I am able to fly. Sometimes I have extra time and am able to do some sketching while I wait, flying and drawing are the two things I love most. I can escape to a world of unlimited freedom"

"That's wonderful, I'd like to see some of your work one of these visits." she exclaimed. "Life can be so pleasant when we enjoy what we're doing. I have always said that if we have unpleasant tasks to perform we can always find ways to make the task more pleasant. Isn't it interesting how such a simple thing as attitude and outlook can be so profound and make such a huge difference in how one feels?"

"Definitely," I answered as I began to dig the hole in the appointed spot.

"When I have unpleasant tasks to do I always try to do the most unpleasant one first. Then I live for what the future has in store.

When you do the unpleasant things first, everything just keeps getting better and better. Doing things this way makes it easy to stay cheerful and pleasant." She paused; "You see, the best is always next."

"That certainly is interesting, but what do you do if you can't do the unpleasant things first, you know that sometimes you just can't?" I questioned.

"That's a very good question! Jonathan," She exclaimed, "I just take the advice of the Seven Dwarfs, I whistle while I work. It is kind of like planting these bushes. First you dig a hole. That is dirty work, it strains the back. It's the hardest part of the job, thank heaven you can do it first. Next you put the proper planting soil mixture in the hole and plant the bushes. This is often stinky and messy but simple and quick. When it is all done, you know that each spring you can look forward to the beautiful blossoms it will bring, the pleasant fragrance. My advice Jonathan, is to live everyday for what the future will bring."

"Yes, it's good to have something to look forward to," I replied, "these bushes will be beautiful for many years to come."

"Well Jonathan, thank you for your help you certainly did a great job. Have a safe trip home." Then once again she repeated the now familiar phrase, *"remember, what you do for others makes you who you are."*

As I flew home I thought about the bushes and how the results of the work we accomplished today will be manifested for years to come. That was certainly a new way of looking at things, I really had never thought about life in this way before. The things you do each day remain as a testament that you had been there that you were an active part of life. For many years to come I could look at the bushes and I will forever be a small part of each spring, even when I've moved on those bushes will remain. Could that have been what she meant when she advised me to *"live every day for what the future will bring?"*

The visits were always interesting. I was always wondering what I would learn next. On this particular trip to the ranch house as I approached the house I could see Miss Hollings sitting on the porch. She was in her chair, wheeled up next to a table. There was another chair and what appeared to be lemonade on the table. She sat there balancing her checkbook.

"Hello Miss Hollings, would you like me to put the package on the table?" I asked energetically.

"Yes, thank you very much Jonathan," she answered.

I placed the package on the table and when I returned she had poured the lemonade. Invitingly she said, "Please have a chair and enjoy some fresh made lemonade with me,"

"Thank you," I responded. "Miss Hollings, I would prefer if you called me Johnny."

"Certainly," she replied. "You can call me Sarah."

"Oh No ma'am, I couldn't do that!" I quickly exclaimed.

"Your mother certainly raised you well. Then would you please just call me Miss H," she insisted.

"I can do that, Miss H," I said agreeing.

"Johnny," she said, "Life can be so interesting at times. Have you ever noticed how every event in a person's life can either have a positive or a negative effect on them?"

"Not really," I said. Here she started again with one of her life analogies that always seemed to make perfect sense and caused me to ponder.

She continued; "It's like this check book. Every transaction changes the checkbook with either a plus or a minus. Life has it's own checkbook too. However, the unique thing about life's checkbook is; *you* decide if the transactions will either be positive or negative in your life's check register. Some people walk around with a huge negative balance, others with a huge positive balance, but most just have enough to survive. Life is full of obstacles. Each hurdle is determined to slow you down or even stop you. The real challenge is to face each obstacle and turn every experience into something useful, one from which you can grow in some way. There is always a way you can make a positive entry in your checkbook even out of life's bitter moments."

I listened, pondering *my* "life's checkbook." I certainly had many bitter moments growing up and was sure I had a big negative balance. I listened intently as she counseled me on life.

"It is one of life's challenges to make a positive out of what many would consider to be a negative. You are happiest when you make as many positive entries as possible. You have to take the initiative and make it happen. It is a great feeling to have conquered life's negative with a positive!" she advised, "Johnny, you can be either a positive or a negative in the equation of life and you choose which one."

Her words were always so powerful and succinct. I wondered how much of my life I had chosen a negative entry over a positive one. Could I really make a difference in my own life, I mean me?

Then she said something that really made me think, "Johnny, a very interesting thing about life's checkbook, we can always change past negatives to positives."

We continued to talk about life and it's challenges. There was no doubt that I had contributed to a lot of negative in the past. I could sense that our visit was coming to an end when she began to roll her chair toward the door. "Johnny, thanks for the visit." She never missed thanking me when it was she who seemed to be always giving to me!

She followed me as I made my way to the steps ending our visit with the now increasingly more familiar refrain, "Remember Johnny, *what you do for others makes you who you are.*"

This flight home was very poignant. Her words, *"we can always change past negatives to positives,"* kept echoing in my mind.

"We can always change past negatives to positives," a powerful statement! But is it really true?

Every visit seemed to have some philosophical message that just came mostly spontaneously from everyday life. On some occasions we would sit on the porch and visit while I sketched the beautiful scenery. I looked forward to these visits each Friday with greater anticipation. I always returned feeling uplifted and somehow a little more complete for just having been there. Often I didn't want to leave, but knew I was just a guest, actually a student at the feet of a great teacher.

One particular Friday the routine was the same as usual, however when I sat down at the table she had baked some beautiful cream filled pastries. They were placed on a serving dish in the center of the table. I wondered how was she going to turn these pastries into a lesson of life? Somehow I knew that she would.

"Here, Johnny, please have one," she insisted.

"Thank you I love sweets, especially homemade" I remembered the many time my mom had baked so many great treats for me when I was at home. I took a big bite. What! I wrinkled my nose and I puckered my lips. I made a funny face. They were tart cherry pastries. Although it was very good, I might add, I had never expected tart cherries.

Together we had a good laugh, and then she said invitingly, " Here, have another."

"What will I find this time?" I laughed while leaning forward.

"Maybe a surprise," she quipped.

I took another and once again a new experience. I had prepared myself for the tart cherry taste and wow! That wasn't what I tasted. Again I was surprised with the sweet taste of apple and cinnamon. Once again we had a good laugh at her joke and my facial expressions.

Then she started with her powerful teaching. "It is so easy to prejudge, just like these pastries. We base our judgments on what we expect from the boundaries of our own limited experiences. We take one look at others and we stereotype them.

We've made our judgments before we have given ourselves a chance to get a fair and honest picture. Then we do everything we can to make that judgment right. When you were about to eat the first pastry you were ready for a sweet creamy filling. You had formed an image and expectation of the taste your mouth was watering for and so were your taste buds. However even when you tasted the tart cherry, your brain tried to make it sweet, but your taste buds were just too strong to be fooled. The contrast was so strong it even accentuated the difference"

"You sure fooled me. I had better take a peek before I have another," I said with a smile.

"It is so important," she went on, "whenever you meet another person or whenever you deal with anyone, to withhold judgment until you have all the facts. Or better yet, don't judge at all. Even then, my father used to say 'Sarah, people are generally doing the very best that they can, so give them all the room you can, and give them the benefit of the doubt.'"

"When we prejudge others we find ways to make our judgments right," she advised. "It is one's tendency to look for all the qualities and characteristics to back our perspective, often overlooking many good qualities. The good qualities generally overwhelm and outnumber the not so good ones. And since people are mostly filled with goodness, when we point out their faults we find ourselves looking at others with a very narrow vision."

Our time had gone fast, Miss H started rolling her chair to the door and said, "Remember Johnny, *what you do for others makes you who you are.*"

As I flew home I thought of how many times I had prejudged people and just like the pastries, when I became better acquainted with them I had to make some adjustments in my judgment. She was right, people are mostly good. She made a valid point, -- when you dwell on people's weak points you are working with the more narrow part of that person. She also had said, *"When you focus on the good points of others you always see them at their best, plus you have more to work with: and besides that, when God was finished making everything He declared it to be 'good.'"*

Sam Spencer

Chapter Six

The Experience

The Experience

It happened in mid August, It seemed to be hotter than usual. I don't know why, but this day as I delivered the box to Miss. H. I happened to bring in my drawing tablet just as I had done many times before, but this time would be different. I put the package away and sat down on the sofa for another of our now expected and cherished weekly visits. She had not been talking long when it happened. What I will refer to as the "experience." I was just sitting there with my tablet in hand listening as I had so many times in the past. It came suddenly. It was like my eyes were opened and I could see beyond Miss. H. I mean beyond that chair which confined her movement. I could see her spirit; it was free and full of life. It was as if she had never been captured by that mechanical chair of steel. The chair seemed to have given itself up to a greater power, the power of her spirit.

I could see her in her youthful beauty. The beauty of her naturally curly flowing hair, flowing to just below the shoulders. I saw it to be very dark brown, almost black; there were none of her gray tones. Her eyes were bright and clear, pure and forgiving. Her smile was sweet and innocent, not innocent like a child, but devoid of guile, innocent of being unkind to anyone. She was playful, caring and very alive. She appeared in a flowing springish mid-length light colored lacy gown. She was dancing in the garden and with every turn spreading her special kind of happiness, kindness and peace. I could see her soul, full of understanding, love and compassion for others. Some of these special gifts had even been generously shared with me. She had something to give to everyone and she gave of it freely, without expectation. One needn't ask, if she saw a need, she gave abundantly.

I heard very little of what Miss H said on this visit. I was caught up in this... this trance. She just kept talking. It was something about her father starting the company. I kept drawing. I had never peered into anyone's soul before. Everything I saw was the complete Miss H. I saw her pure honesty, and knew she was someone who could be trusted. She was someone who truly cared about others.

I frantically sketched what was before me. I just kept drawing; I wanted to seize every detail of this vision, this unique perspective. It had to be perfect. I wanted to capture the image of Miss H, this woman that I had learned to admire, this woman who had taught me so much. She just kept talking and I kept drawing.

Miss. H began to roll toward the door, this signaled that our visit was up. No! No! I wanted to stay. I needed to finish. I hadn't captured everything yet. I needed more time! I now would have to finish my work from memory. Could I do it? Could I preserve this vision, the image I had seen? Oh, I hoped so.

As I left, she once again echoed that now very familiar chorus, "Remember, Johnny, *what you do for others makes you who you are.*"

The flight back to the hanger did not dim the vision of Miss. H. The "experience" had fixed a vivid imprint in my mind. I hurried home. My only desire was to portray on canvas what I had seen. Her image was still intense in my mind. Determined to get started I rushed into my apartment and settled in front of my easel. So intense was this image that my need to look at the sketch was rare. Sleep passed me by while being sustained by a drive to complete the portrait. So deep was my obsession with my project that hunger was never a thought. The portrait needed to be perfect. Her image must be preserved forever. It was a labor of love to get every stroke of the brush just right. The painting needed to be finished, dry and ready for my presentation on our next visit. Nothing could stand in the way of this self appointed mission.

Finally, early Monday morning, I had it. My rendering was complete. I had captured the very nature of this woman. I had never respected anyone like this before. I had never acknowledged so much good in anyone before. I had never specifically looked for the good in others. My perspective was always one of defense, one in which I just looked out for myself. This was remarkably different. Had I changed? Was there some type of metamorphosis taking place in me? Was I beginning to look at people from a new perspective? Had I been given some kind of a new understanding? What was this awakening within me? One thing for sure my eyes would never look at Miss. H in the same way again. This experience was changing me. I felt it. A profoundly deeper respect for her was emerging. Perhaps I was experiencing a new type of love. I had not yet realized the depth and impact of this special experience. Everything was all still so fresh on my mind. Soon, however, I would recognize the depth of the impact this would have on my life.

It was good to have a very busy week. People were being shuttled in and out all week. Each day upon returning from work I would sit and appreciate the portrait and imagine presenting it to Miss H. This was my best work ever! My whole soul was put into it. Every day I anxiously anticipated my Friday ritual. My masterpiece would be presented as a genuine gift from my heart. Never had I done anything like this before.

Every gift ever given was more or less given out of self-imposed obligation.   Never much thought, never much effort.   Just something in a box with wrapping paper, and occasionally not even that.   Always being worried about the gift being accepted by the recipient. Was it good enough?   Would I be acknowledged? Every act was always qualified and justified with my own self-enforced conditions.   My disappointment was exacerbated by those very self-imposed conditions.   How measured were all my past actions.

I recognized that this might very well be the first real pure gift that ever came from my heart.   A profound awareness of being unconditionally connected to someone encompassed me!   An overwhelming feeling of gratitude, true gratitude filled my heart.   Up to now in my life my gratitude was just what had been learned from the warden, I was compelled so I did.   This felt so good.   My attitude was so positive, I found myself liking everybody.   People didn't seem to bother me, I found myself having more patience with others.   This actually felt that I was a very likable person emerging.   I found myself skipping and whistling all day both physically and mentally.   It was the first time in my life I had a feeling that I in fact liked myself.   Could this truly selfless act have done all that?

Finally It was Friday, "special delivery" day. I was bouncing around like a child on Christmas Eve. Early morning found me in the art store choosing the perfect frame for the portrait. The frame was elegant, gold in color with floral sculptures in the corners. In spite of it's quality and beauty somehow it didn't seem worthy of it's recipient. The clerk helped me pick out an oak easel as a permanent mounting place for my gift. Miss H could place the easel in her living room by the corner of the window. With the portrait on the easel it would be a reminder that she was a masterpiece in progress.

This was my day, my special day. Lots of sunshine would be made today and made by me! Sunshine not only for myself but also for Miss H. This was going to be a genuine gift of myself, given in a way like never before. I was going to share the very best of myself with Miss H. Words cannot express the excitement and euphoria that filled my spirit. This was without doubt the largest deposit I had ever made in my life's checkbook. I liked how it made me feel!

Now to the hangar for the final preparations. The easel was placed on the floor behind the seats. Carefully I put the painting in the plane on the seat next to me. Everything was ready. Finally to retrieve the package. I looked everywhere. There was no package to be found. Who dropped the ball? This was like a ritual, not only for me but also for the company. The package was always there, waiting for me. It never failed. What happened? Where was it?

In desperation I called my supervisor, "Mack, I can't find the package for Miss. Hollings," I said frantically, "I've looked everywhere and it is almost 12:30. What should I do? Where is it?"

Mack began to speak slower and softer than usual, "There won't be any trip for you today, Miss. H was admitted to the hospital late last night."

"What happened? What is going on? How is she? Will she be okay?" I franticly interrupted.

"All I know is that the doctors are not allowing any visitors, they've put her in the ICU. I don't know any more than that, you can go home, there will be no flight today," he responded.

I quickly became very frightened. I rushed to the hospital. My interrogations yielded no more than what Mack had already advised me. He was right; no one was allowed to see her. How could this be happening to me? It wasn't right. This wasn't what I wanted for today. This was *my* special day. I had made plans. All I could do was just wait. There was no news late into the night. Finally about midnight I went to my apartment to rest.

Early Saturday morning I hurried back to the hospital. Arriving shortly after 7:00 a.m. I hurried to the nursing station and inquired, "How is Miss Hollings? What can you tell me?"

"Are you family?" she questioned.

"No, just a close friend. Has there been any change overnight?" I asked.

"Oh sir, I am sorry to tell you," she spoke sympathetically, "Miss Hollings passed away about two hours ago. You will have to contact her family for more information. I'm sorry, I'm really sorry."

My eyes began to well up. "No! No! I won't weep, not me," I yelled in my mind. A great emptiness consumed me. I had been betrayed. How could she do this to me? I had a special gift for her. I had put my whole self into this masterpiece my best work ever and she would never be able to see it. The beautiful smile she shared was gone, gone forever, the smile I would never see accepting my first sincere act of kindness. All Sarah had ever done for me were pure and sincere acts of kindness. It was like my whole world had ended. I didn't know how to handle this.

I stopped for breakfast on my way home. Food did nothing for me. My day was spent sitting in my apartment and staring at the portrait. I couldn't stop thinking about the gift I was never going to be able to give. I had so looked forward to this event. Flashbacks of our conversations kept going through my head. I had never experienced such deep despair. I was so empty. I had never lost a friend before, I mean a true friend, someone who I had truly loved. I had never let anyone really be my friend before nor had I ever let anyone love me or should I say I had never let myself be loved by the many others who had tried. But more importantly I had never allowed myself to actually love another person.

Sunday morning came. I got up early and from my apartment window watched the sunrise. Many warm memories went through my mind. I remembered the conversations we had about her enjoying the sunrises. *"You make your own sunshine,"* she had said. Could there be any sunshine that I could make out of this? Was there any way I could make a positive out of this experience as she had taught me? How could I possibly make a positive entry in my life's checkbook?

I dressed and went for a drive. I needed to ponder. As I drove I noticed people entering a church. Memories went through my mind of how my parents had taken me to church with them when I was younger. I remembered the peace and serenity I had always felt sitting in church. I hadn't been inside a church since I'd left home. For some reason I found myself joining the gathering. I went inside and sat down. I didn't even know what kind of church I was in. It wasn't important. Somehow it didn't matter; I just felt the need to be there.

The message from the minister was about forgiveness. Forgiving others, and forgiving oneself.

"To err is human, to forgive is divine," he said. "It takes a special person to forgive the big offenses, and attitudes get more and more bitter the longer one waits to forgive." He made sense. "When you hold a grudge against another," he went on, "it is like a log jam on the river or building a dam with your anger. All that you could have done with that relationship is being held back until you forgive and take away the obstructions. Soon all of your relationships are affected"

I could see how I had held many grudges against those who guided my childhood. I thought of the warden. No matter what he had done I would judge it to be wrong, sure I accepted it, I had to. I kept building this huge logjam one grudge at a time. My frustrations spilled over to my adoptive mom and dad. I had never accepted them wholly as a part of my life. I had been wrong, so wrong! It wasn't like I had some huge hatred. It was as though I had required myself to have an immediate grudge against others. That's what I had learned at the beginning from others at the orphanage. Or that was the lesson I let myself be taught. I was just glad that was in my past. I guess being gone from where I grew up enabled me to block out the parts of my past that I didn't like. But I could tell they were still there, impeding my progress.

"You must let go of the things in the past that stop you from moving forward," the minister kept going. "When you forgive you take away the debris and the obstructions and allow a free flowing relationship with yourself and others."

I had never looked at it that way before. In fact I had never looked at what part I played in anyone's life but my own. How selfish! How self-centered! It was so clear that I needed to let go of the past and remove the debris and move forward.

"If each person in this meeting now would completely forgive one other person today, what a more complete life you would have, what a marvelous community we would enjoy," he continued. "Resolve to take the first step today, don't wait for others, just make up your mind and go forward. Choose one you can handle then move up to the more difficult ones, but begin today!"

The meeting was over. It had given me much food for thought and added so many more emotions, and so many more questions. I just needed to contemplate all that had transpired these last few days. I needed some time to meditate and once again find myself.

Chapter Seven

The Funeral

The Funeral

It was a beautiful early fall morning. Just as the sun began to rise in the east the graveside service began. This was what Miss H had asked for. And most fitting, she was always talking about the beautiful sunrises, sunshine and new beginnings. Perhaps this was a new beginning for her, in a place where she would dance and walk once again. She would be missed.

There appeared to be several hundred people at the service to honor Miss H. I knew only the few people that I had directly worked with at the company. As the sun continued to peek over the horizon I could not help but ponder our precious visits. This was certainly in the style of Miss. H. It was a though Sarah was giving us one final message that with every sunrise comes a new beginning. Certainly for her this was a new beginning. She was now free, well, at least in my view she would be free. Sarah had never allowed herself to be imprisoned in that wheel chair. She never saw herself as handicapped. In fact she had always been her own person, spreading her special sunshine everywhere.

I made my way to the front. I wanted to be as close to her as I could. She had made such an impact on me during our short time together. I was a better person for having known her, yes, a much better person. I just needed to be as close as possible to her right now. She had taught me so much from our visits. One thing for certain I had found someone whom I could trust, someone who seemed to be able to say exactly what I needed to hear in a way that inspired me to listen. She would be sorely missed!

As I approached the front I could see the casket placed over the large hole in the ground. This would be her final resting place. A large spray of flowers adorned the top of the walnut casket; the brass trim was polished to perfection. Several large bouquets of flowers surrounded the stand that supported her. It was all so peaceful and warm. As I moved my eyes to the right I saw a headstone, the inscription read:

James Willis Hollings

Loving Husband and Father

Born   March 18, 1934

Died November, 8 1983

A man who gave to everyone

Next to him I saw the grave of her mother, I read the engraving on the headstone:

Elizabeth Ann Hollings

Loving Wife and Mother

Born   December 2, 1936

Died November, 8 1983

The good woman behind a good man

Had they died together in some kind of accident?   My eyes finally fixed a little further to the right noticing one more headstone in this family plot. This one read:

James Willis Hollings, Jr.

Loving Son and Brother

Born   May 12, 1960

Died November, 8 1983

Taken in his youth

Certainly there had been some tragedy on that day that took the lives of Sarah's family. Now I understood why she lived alone. Her brother was barely 23 years old when he died, that's exactly my age I thought. She was now able to take her place next to her father and be with her family after all these years. They were together again, somewhere. I was certain she was dancing and singing in some celestial garden. Her long dark brown hair would be bouncing as she moved. Perhaps she was even wearing that flowing springish mid-length light colored lacy gown that I had portrayed her in. Yes, Sarah was free! Perhaps even like my painting.

I respectfully walked up to the casket and placed my painting on the easel by the head of the casket. I then fixed a single rose in the top left corner. For a moment I gazed upon the casket, wiped back a tear as I took a few steps backward to remain as close as possible, but just out of the way.

The minister spoke some comforting words, two other people gave short talks and a few songs were sung. I heard little as I relived the precious visits which now, with each thought, became increasingly more priceless. I had been given a treasure. I wanted to guard it with my life. And I recognized that it was given to me freely, I had done nothing to earn it. All she had given me was truly an unconditional gift.

I thought of her with no family to carry on her warm feelings, what of her heritage? Would she be like me, no heritage to look back on, with no one to carry forward her greatness? I turned and saw the throng of people moving toward me and toward the casket. Each passing by the casket one by one with many of them placing a flower on it. I began to sense that they knew what I knew. This woman had touched many lives. She had shared with many who lived in rain filled overcast lives, the sunshine she created each day. Not only making enough for herself, but also sufficient to share with everyone with whom she came in contact.

I was beginning to understand who she really was, and what she had accomplished as she sat in that chair day after day for those many years. Your heritage is not simply your family. Your heritage is you! It's what you leave behind when you're gone and all that is left is your memory. It is the seeds that you plant, the lives you touch. It is truly what you do for others. That is just what she was telling me. I was he who could make the difference. A little of Sarah's heritage was in all the people who passed by the casket that beautiful morning and undoubtedly many others who were not there. Her heritage lived on in each one of them, and perhaps, hopefully... even in me! She didn't need family to carry on her tradition; she had so many people to perpetuate her immense legacy. She let everyone be a part of her family.

By now most of the people had withdrawn. I found myself still standing pondering. Wondering, what next? A well-dressed, distinguished looking gentleman with slightly graying hair came to stand beside me.

"You're Jonathan Grant aren't you?" He asked.

"Yes," I answered, in an inquisitive tone.

"I'm Mr. Martin, my father was the 'M' in H&M Minerals. Dad was a one-third partner in the company. Sarah's mom and dad had the rest," he continued. "Sarah was quite a woman. Every one of us was proud to have worked for her. You see, after that terrible plane crash that took the lives of the rest of her family she began to run this company even from her hospital bed. She was the sole survivor. Unfortunately she was paralyzed from the waist down from the accident, but that never slowed Sarah down. She has done an outstanding job running this company. Every Friday you would deliver the reports so she could make the decisions we needed her to make. Thanks for a job well done!"

Many unanswered questions were now beginning brought to light. I listened as he continued. "After she got out of the hospital she would leave at 12:30 every Friday afternoon to return to the ranch. Mr. H would fly his own plane, but for Sarah we employed a pilot to keep up the family tradition. She insisted on flying in spite of the accident. That was Sarah, meeting every one of life's challenges without hesitation. Eventually it was too hard on her weak heart to make the trip so we would send her the weekly reports by plane each Friday at 12:30 this too so she could carry on the family tradition. She would say that it helped her keep a living memory of her father each Friday when the plane would deliver her the package. She would always thank me when it was she who did so much for all of us. You performed a valuable service for her young man, I thank you in her behalf."

He continued to speak of Sarah with reverence and admiration. "She reached out to all the employees of this company. She believed that everyone was a person of great potential and that if you just treated him or her with that kind of respect, they would more easily attain their potential. She really admired you young man. You reminded her so much of her brother. He was about your age when he died, Jim was also my friend."

"Thank you." I said. I didn't know what else to say.

"Oh, by the way she asked me to deliver to you this letter personally if she didn't pull through the operation," he said as he handed me a sealed envelope. "And if you could, I would like you to stop in at my office tomorrow morning at 10:00, will that work?"

"Sure, and thank you," I said again. What else could I say?

We shook hands and he left. Immediately I opened the letter and began to read it as I walked back to my car.

Dear Johnny,

When I first watched you get out of the plane earlier this spring, I saw a young man who within him were his own seeds of greatness. I saw a young man who was confident but very cautious. A young man with dreams yet lacked vision. I saw a young man with power in him that was being held back by the past, and perhaps he needed a jump-start. I saw a little of my younger brother in you and many seeds of greatness that had not yet been sown. Perhaps you are not even aware of what is within you.

However, it is all in there and only you can let it come into being. Remember when you prejudge others you are right. At least once you make your judgment, you will do all you can to prove your own decision right. Your verdict places limitations on the person you judge. Don't prejudge others not even yourself. Remove barriers Johnny, don't erect them! Be all that is in you!

Have a passion for life! Live for what tomorrow will bring. Paint your own picture of what you want for your life. Remember that every new sunrise opens a new day, a new beginning, and you decide if you will let the sunshine in or shut it out. Remember Johnny, when there is no sunshine, you must make your own sunshine. Always choose to be a plus in the equation of life, you will find greater happiness there.

Sometimes we refuse to let ourselves be loved. Give yourself permission to be loved, give yourself permission to love yourself.

Give yourself permission to love others. You must first be able to love yourself, and then you can truly love others.

Life in this chair has been a great blessing for me. I have been able to see people for what they can become rather than what they are at this moment. I have been able to see them for their potential rather than just performance. Each person's performance is just an indicator of where they are today. Perhaps as I looked beyond my own limitations I also have been able to see beyond the limitations that others have placed on themselves. Look beyond your limitations and don't limit yourself.

Remember Johnny, what you do for others makes you who you are. Be sure that you do for others as the person you envision *yourself to be. Do for them as if you were already who you will become. See the world and others through the special eyes that all of us have been given, those eyes which see into the soul, that see who someone really is and all the goodness they can become. Paint this true image in your minds eye of who they really are and then the way that you see them is how you must treat them.*

Forever your Friend.

Love,

Sarah

Tears rolled down my cheeks. This was the first time I ever remember really crying. I had never felt like that before. I not only felt loved for who I was, but for what I could be. Sarah's love was truly unconditional. It still lived even beyond the grave. Her faith in me was overwhelming. Her vision of what I could be was humbling. That was the first time in my life I had ever experienced so much emotion regarding others and myself. As I looked at others, I began to see them differently. It was as though I was now magically seeing them through Sarah's eyes, with a new insight that she had endowed upon me. And now, the special person who had helped me find this extraordinary treasure was gone. I would neither be able to thank her nor sit again at her tutelage.

I wanted to be the person whom she felt I could be. On a few occasions I think I had experienced that person, so I knew that he was in there. How could I let him out? Often Sarah would say that I had all it takes to become all I wanted to be. Was she right? Did I actually have all that potential and resources already within me? If so, how could I unleash them? How could I now be anything less than how Sarah saw me?

Sam Spencer

Chapter Eight

The Awakening

The Awakening

The next morning, slightly before 10:00 a.m. I approached Mr. Martin's secretary. I had never spent much time in the office. Actually I had only been there one time before and that was for my preliminary job interview. All the other time I had spent at the company airstrip and at the office by the hangar. I didn't remember the people were so friendly the first time I had been here; perhaps I was too nervous and preoccupied. Perhaps I was too caught up in myself.

I was invited to wait in Mr. Martin's office. It was large. Not only was there a large desk, but also a large conference table with a dozen chairs around it. The conference table was clean and the only thing on it was one large envelope. Mr. Martin's desk had several stacks of folders and papers on it. I was sure he was quite busy. This will be quick, I thought. I wondered if I was going to be fired, or more politely... laid off? I noticed that my name was hand written on the large envelope. I wondered what it was. I was curious but I wouldn't dare touch it. Were these my marching orders? Soon I would find out.

As I continued to look around the room I was shocked to see hanging on the wall my portrait of Sarah. This was quite amazing and also puzzling. To the right I saw another large portrait. As I approached to inspect the artwork my attention was drawn to a plaque under the portrait. There was a nameplate that read:

James Willis Hollings

This was Sarah's father, I recognized him from some of the photos at the ranch house. Under the nameplate was another brass plaque which had an inscription that read:

"What you do for others makes you who you are."

-- James W. Hollings

This was the same statement Sarah had spoken so many times; they were the words of her father! Just then Mr. Martin entered and said, "If you had known Mr. Hollings, you would have known where Sarah got her personality. He was a good, fair man. That phrase has become our company slogan. After every interview, after every meeting, many times a day Mr. Hollings would repeat those words to everyone. Sarah believed them too. She lived them and followed in her father's great tradition."

I remembered the words well. I had heard them many times. She had ended every visit with them. Now I knew more of why, she truly was carrying on the tradition of her father's legacy. They seemed to have an ever-expanding meaning as I learned more about my dear friend.

"I hope you don't mind my placing your portrait next to his," he continued, "you captured the very essence of how I remember her before the accident. You may take it with you if you would like."

"No! I'm honored, please keep it next to her father." was my reply not knowing what else to say. "I'm sure they are together now."

"That portrait will continue to keep her memory alive and to add sunshine into our lives," returned Mr. Martin. "Thank you."

Mr. Martin then invited me to sit at the conference table. He took a seat across from me and began once again to speak, "Sarah really liked you young man. She would say, 'I see a great young man in this boy, he is just trying to find out who he is and what he wants from life.' She would also say that you reminded her of her brother. You may not know that he was about your age when he died."

"I can see that Sarah has touched many lives," I interjected. "I could not believe how many people came to her funeral."

"Yes," Mr. Martin went on, "Even though she had a weak heart in medical terms, it was strong spiritually and emotionally. At times it seemed to be as big as the whole world. She touched many lives and helped countless people. Often she would say to me, 'some times all a person needs is a jump start.' And then she would find a way to help give them some kind of a 'jump start.'" As he stood up he said, "Sarah had something special she wanted me to present to you." He opened the drawer in his desk and pulled out a set of keys.

I remained seated, not certain what to do. He then motioned me over to the large window at the rear of his office. From three stories up I could see the airstrip just beyond a row of tall trees. He pointed to the hangar on the airstrip and placed the keys in my hand. That plane out there is yours, Sarah wanted you to have it."

"What? You're kidding?" I questioned. "There is no way this could be true!"

"No, that was the way she wanted it. The plane is yours, our plan is to contract for your services." He spoke with firmness. "Maybe she intended this to be your 'jump start', I'm not sure."

"Oh, Thank you! Thank you! I just don't know what else to say," I spoke quietly but with modest excitement. I felt myself beginning to get emotional. I swallowed hard as I fought back the tears of joy and humility, this tear thing was happening much too often. I couldn't show this kind of emotion in front of anyone. That wasn't me. And to think of it, crying twice in one week. I definitely didn't want to start anything. Nobody had ever expressed so much confidence in me nor showed so much love or interest in me, at least not to my recognition.

"I have the paperwork Sarah had prepared in the envelope on the table," he said as he handed me the envelope from the conference table. "Please look these over and we can discuss them later."

We each said good-bye and I went straight to this incredible gift. How could anybody have so much trust in me, so much confidence to give me such a gift? Why was Sarah so giving, and to me? Did she truly see me as someone special? I sat in the plane wiping down the instruments and seats like a hundred times before, but this time was different. This plane was mine. I would make the most of this opportunity to honor Sarah. I noticed an old easel I kept in the plane behind the seat, thoughts of the portrait flooded my mind. My gift to Sarah. I never had the opportunity to give it to her. My emotions finally overcame me; I could hold them no longer. Tears rolled down my cheeks as my thoughts revisited the past. Now I would never be able to show my gratitude to Sarah for all that she had taught me or for what she had given me. She had truly walked her talk; she lived by every word she spoke. Her kind gentle way was so overpowering even from the grave. Was this what a legacy is all about?

As I sat in the plane I took her letter out of my pocket and began to read it again. Had she really seen so much in me? Perhaps even enough to earn such a trust? I thought about what I had just read in her letter. As I pondered I realized that I prejudged so many people and I was the one who lost out. My thoughts turned to my foster parents. I had placed them into a stereotype and had not allowed them to love me. Or maybe it is better said, that I accepted little of their love. I had made no entries in life's checkbook. I could plainly see that I had not given myself permission to be loved. Even my adoptive parents I had treated the same even though they were especially good to me. I realized that everything I had ever wanted was right there in front of me all the time. I had clearly not accepted it. Playing catch with my father. The pie and homemade ice cream that my mother and grandmother had made for me. Family outings and times spent together. My eyes were opened to a new vision, an understanding of all the goodness that I had not accepted from others. All the love that was mine to receive. This was not the legacy that I wanted to leave behind. Somehow I needed to make some changes. And I needed to start now! How could I make a positive entry from my past?

Sarah was right! *"What you do for others makes you who you are."* I had never trusted. I didn't give others a chance. I had not allowed myself to be loved and I had not given love to others. My focus in life had been mainly focused on myself. I had placed limitations on others and myself just as the minister had said. It was becoming evident to me that I was the one who was in charge of who I was going to become. I was in charge of building up or tearing down. I was in charge of how I would treat others. I was in charge of how I would accept or reject others. It was time to begin living for the future, building something of value.

The future was going to be better, the best that I could make it. All positive deposits, my own heritage, a legacy of doing for others! Wow, just thinking this way brought back the excited feelings I had as I worked on Sara's painting.

Chapter Nine

The

Transformation

The Transformation

I took a few days off. There were a few things I needed to do. I packed a small suitcase and filed a flight plan for Middleton. All the way there I thought about the many things I had missed or actually the many things I hadn't taken advantage of or accepted. It had been almost five years since I left home. It was wrong of me to have been gone so long and not have maintained any regular contact with my parents. It is amazing how distorted you view life becomes with even a little anger and contempt guiding you. I grew up being angry with everyone and everything. It was time I finally became an adult, showing real maturity. Giving up my anger. It did me no good. I needed to forgive and forget, then accept. I needed to look forward and not behind. I realized that it took the loss of Sarah to get me to see what was mine all the time. I wasn't going to lose any more of my precious life! She was right; it was all there all the time. I had not allowed myself to participate. I was beginning to awaken to the fact that the best gift that Sarah had given me was not the keys to this airplane, but a vision of what my heritage could be, of who I could become. What I could leave behind. She had given me the keys to being the genuine and sincere Jonathan Christian Grant. Yes, she had given me special keys, the keys that unlocked the door to being the best I could ever be. Yes! This was her greatest gift.

As I landed at the airfield where I first worked a rush of good memories flooded my mind. I visited briefly with a few old friends as I waited for my taxi. Upon leaving we shook hands as I found myself repeating the phrase; "Remember, *what you do for others makes you who you are.*"

 I was on a mission and wanted to waste no time until I had completed this self-imposed commission. "Please, take me to a flower shop," I ordered the driver.

"Surely", he responded.

As we drove I must have sounded preachy. "You never know what you have until you lose it," I said. "A person can go through life and never notice what is out there. So much can pass you by unnoticed and unappreciated. It is kind of like driving on this road. I have gone to and from this airport many times and never really consciously looked to see what was there." I just kept talking. I must have sounded like Sarah and that would be just fine!

"Here's the flower shop," the driver said as he pulled into the drive.

"Please wait, while I get some flowers," I said as I bolted from the car.

I purchased two large bouquets of flowers, one to be delivered to Grandma C's house, the other I took back to the car. "234 Grant Ave." I said. "I have some sunshine I need to make today!"

As we continued the ride I recited to the driver the well-known phrase which would soon become my creed too, *"What you do for others make you who you are."* I continued speaking with a confession and a promise, "With that rule to measure my life by, and based on what I've done for others... in the past, I can't count for much, ···yet. I truly have made myself who I am! But you can be sure of this, things are about to change!"

As the driver stopped in front of the house I felt another rush of fond memories. "Have a great day," I said as I paid the driver and he drove away.

Here I am, standing on the sidewalk in front of the house where I was raised. Memories, increasingly more precious, and only good ones occupied my mind, in fact they all now seemed good.

As I unlatched the gate I whispered out loud, "Mom, Dad, I've come home to give, to love and to let myself be loved. I've come home to live for what the future will bring. I've come home to be who I always could have been. I've come home to be a positive in my life's equation. I've come home to build my heritage. I've come home to do for you and thereby become my very best!"

I paused and with a tear in my eye, I promised, "Grandma, you're next, I just hope I'm not too late!" This was my new beginning. Today I was not only going to make some of my own sunshine, but more than that, today I would first start with making my own magnificent sunrise.

I knocked on the door, I knew what I wanted, and I knew where I wanted to go. I knew who I wanted to become. And I knew it was all inside of me. I have a great and clear vision; I would now be that person!

As the doorknob began to move my emotions creep to the surface and I whispered out loud; "Sarah, Thanks for this great awakening, such a wonderful gift!"

The Awakening

Sam Spencer

www.ingramcontent.com/pod-product-compliance
Lightning Source LLC
Chambersburg PA
CBHW070602180626
46817CB00005B/1959

* 9 7 8 1 9 3 8 0 9 1 0 0 1 *